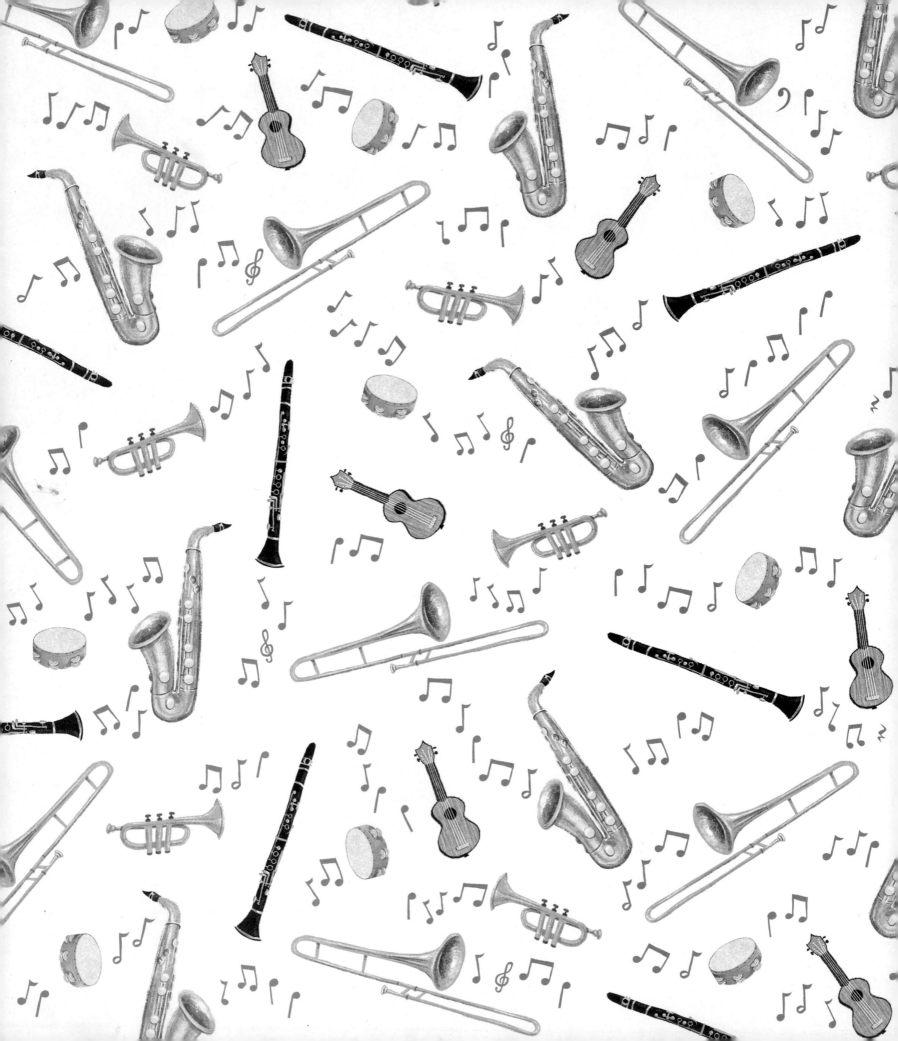

For my daughter (who helped me find this story) – G.P.J.

For my wife Annette and daughters, Emily, Grace and Olivia – J.H.

Farshore

First published in Great Britain 2021 by Farshore

An imprint of HarperCollins*Publishers*
1 London Bridge Street, London SE1 9GF
www.farshore.co.uk

HarperCollins*Publishers*
1st Floor, Watermarque Building, Ringsend Road
Dublin 4, Ireland

Text copyright © Gareth P. Jones 2021
Illustrations copyright © Jeff Harter 2021
Gareth P. Jones and Jeff Harter have asserted their moral rights.

ISBN 978 1 4052 9432 4

Printed in China

1

A CIP catalogue record for this title is available from the British Library.

THE
LION
ON THE
BUS

BY GARETH P. JONES
ILLUSTRATED BY JEFF HARTER

Farshore

The wheels on the bus go round and round,
round and round, round and round.
The wheels on the bus go round and round,

ALL DAY LONG!

THE PARK

BUS
STOP

L

The lion on the bus goes, "Rar-Rar-Rar!

Rar-Rar-Rar!

RAR-RAR-RAR!"

The lion on the bus goes, "RAR-RAR-RAR!"

ALL DAY LONG!

The driver on the bus goes beep-beep-beep!

Beep-beep-beep!

BEEP-BEEP-BEEP!

The driver on the bus goes

BEEP-BEEP-BEEP!

ALL DAY LONG!

The people in the street all wave hello,
wave hello, wave hello.

The people in the street all wave hello,
ALL DAY LONG!

The panther on the bus goes . . .

... prowl-prowl-prowl! Prowl-prowl-prowl! PROWL-PROWL-PROWL!

The panther on the bus goes PROWL-PROWL-PROWL, ALL DAY LONG!

The crocodile on the bus goes,

"Snap-snap-snap! Snap-snap-snap!
SNAP-SNAP-SNAP!"

The wolves on the bus go,

"Howl, howl, h–o–w–o–o–o–l!

Howl, howl, h–o–w–o–o–o–l!
Howl, howl, h–o–w–o–o–o–l!"

The wolves on the bus go,

"HOWL, HOWL, H-O-W-O-O-O-O-L!"

ALL DAY LONG!

The driver on the bus goes, "I'm too scared!

I'm too scared!

I'M TOO SCARED!"

The driver on the bus goes,

"I'M TOO SCARED!"

TO THE PARK

ALL DAY LONG!

The people on the bus scream,

"Please don't bite!
Please don't bite!
PLEASE DON'T BITE!"

The people on the bus scream,

"PLEASE DON'T BITE!"

ALL DAY LONG!

Then the lion,
and the **crocodile**,
and the **panther**,
and the **wolves**
on the bus all open wide,

open wide,
OPEN WIDE.

Then the lion, and the panther,
and the crocodile, and the wolves
on the bus **all open wide,**

ALL . . .

. . . TOGETHER NOW!

"A ONE! A TWO!
A ONE, TWO, THREE, FOUR!"

DOO-WOP-BEE-DOOO!
DOO-WOP-BEE-DOOO!
DOO-WOP-BEE-DOOO!

TO THE PARK

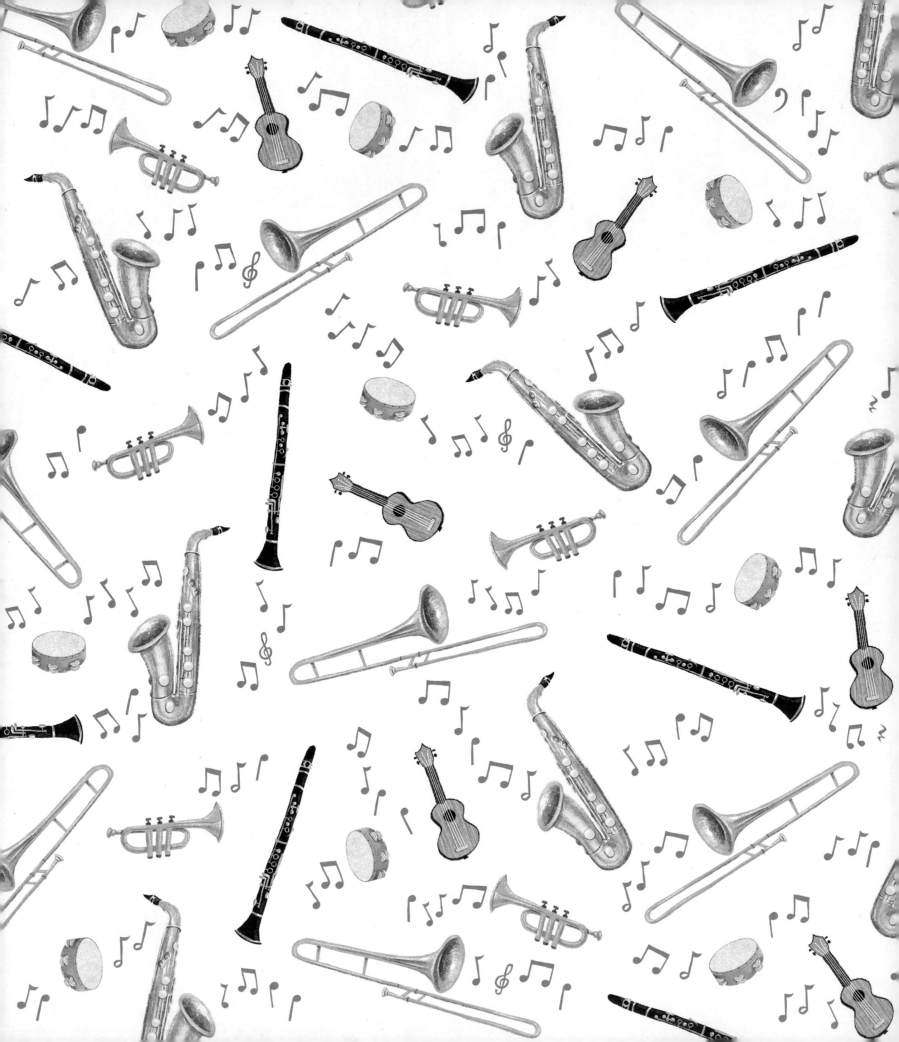